For Charley, Daniel, Annie
and all their boats

K.H.

For Barnaby and Augusta

P.B.

First published 1995 by
Walker Books Ltd
87 Vauxhall Walk
London SE11 5HJ

This edition published 2008

10 9 8 7 6 5 4 3 2

Text © 1995 Kathy Henderson
Illustrations © 1995 Patrick Benson

This book has been typeset in Columbus.

Printed in China

British Library Cataloguing in Publication Data
A catalogue record for this book is
available from the British Library.

ISBN 978-1-4063-1335-2

www.walkerbooks.co.uk

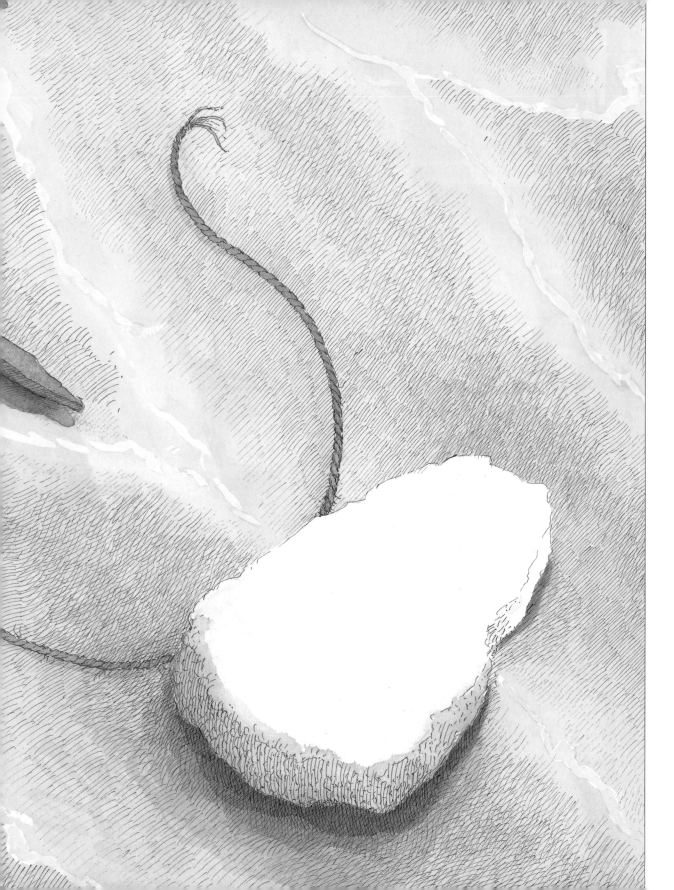

THE LITTLE BOAT

written by

KATHY HENDERSON

illustrated by

PATRICK BENSON

WALKER BOOKS
AND SUBSIDIARIES
LONDON · BOSTON · SYDNEY · AUCKLAND

Down by the shore
where the sea meets the land
licking at the pebbles
sucking at the sand
and the wind flaps
the sunshades
and the ice-cream man
out-shouts the seagulls
and the people come
with buckets and spades
and suntan lotion
to play on the shore
by the edge of the ocean

a little boy
made himself a boat
from an old piece
of polystyrene plastic
with a stick for a mast
and a string tail sail
and he splashed
and he played
with the boat he'd made
digging it a harbour
scooping it a creek
all day long by the edge
of the sea
singing
'We are unsinkable
my boat and me!'

until he turned his back
and a small wind blew
and the little boat drifted
away from the shore
out of his reach
across the waves
past the swimmers
and air beds
away from the beach

on sailed the little boat

all alone

and the further it sailed

the bigger grew

the ocean

until all around

was sea

and not a sign of land

not a leaf

not a bird

not a sound

just the wind

and heaving sliding

gliding breathing water

under endless sky

and hours went by
and days went by
and still the little boat
sailed on
with once a glimpse
of the lights from an oil rig
standing in the distance
on giant's legs
and sometimes
the shape of a ship
like a toy
hanging in the air
at the rim of the world

or a bit of driftwood
or rubbish passing
otherwise nothing
on and on

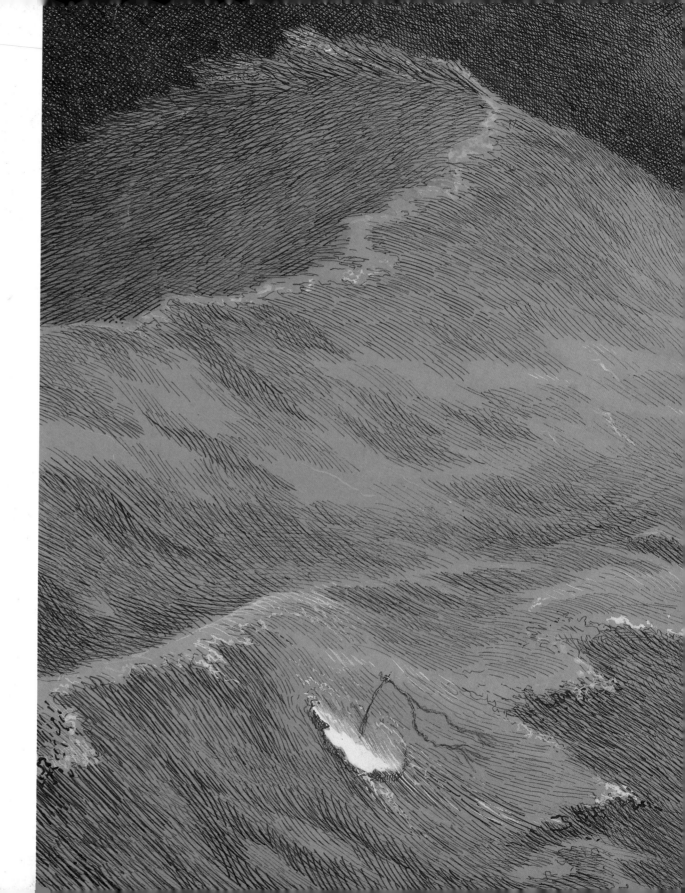

and then came a day
when the sky went dark
and the seas grew uneasy
and tossed about
and the wind
that had whispered
began to roar
and the waves grew bigger
and lashed and tore
and hurled great manes
of spray
in the air
like flames in a fire

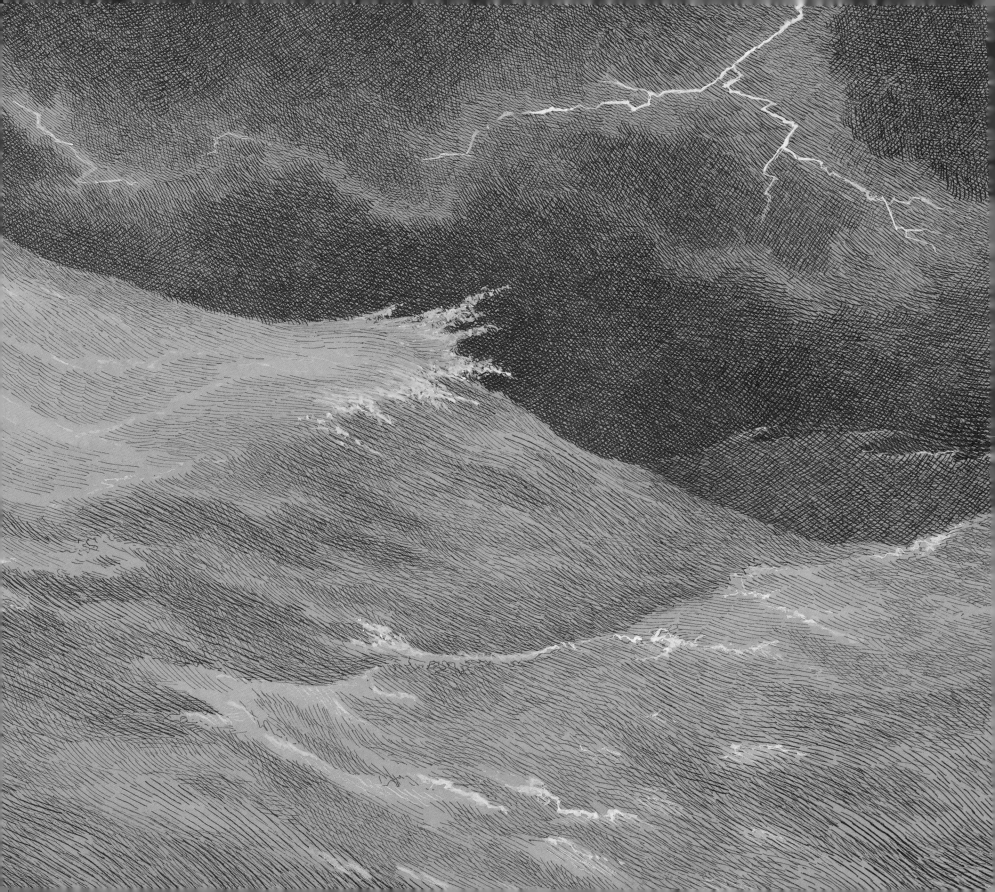

and all night long
as the seas grew rougher
the little boat danced
with the wind
and the weather
till the morning came
and the storm was over
and all was calm and still
and quiet again

and it grabbed the boat
and dived

deep

deep

deep

down

to where the light grows dim
in the depths of the sea
a world of fins and claws
and slippery things
and rocks and wrecks
of ancient ships
and ocean creatures
no one's seen

where
finding that plastic
wasn't food
the fish spat out
the boat again
and up it flew
up up up up
like the flight of an arrow
towards the light
burst through the silver skin
of the sea
and floated on
in the calm sunshine

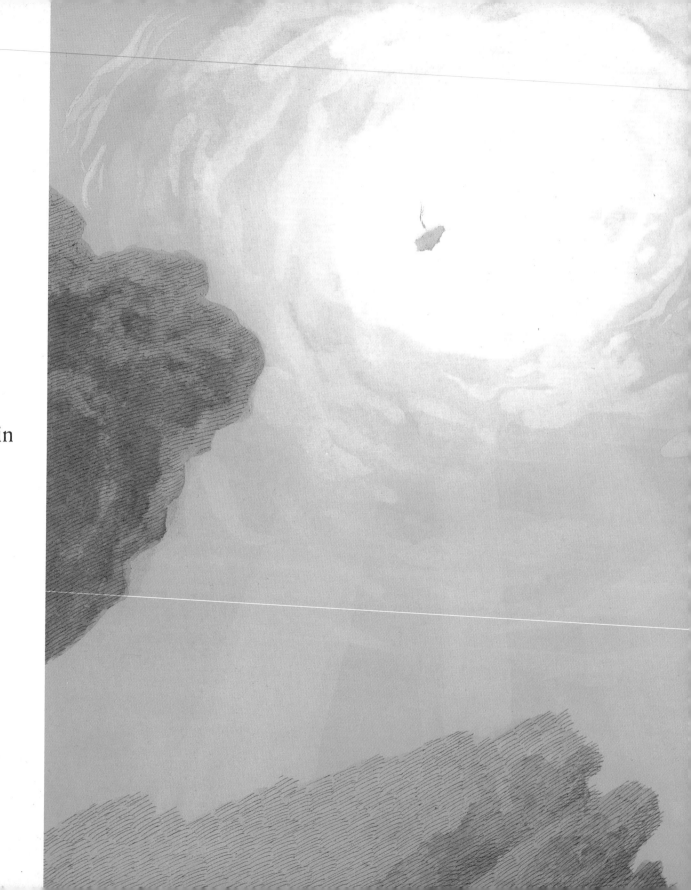

'We are unsinkable
my boat and me!'